Invasion of the Dinner Ladies

HELMSDALE PRIMARY
SUTHERLAND

SEAFISH SURPRISE

Michaela Morgan and Dee Shulman

Collins

JUMBO JETS

First published by A&C Black (Publishers) Ltd 1997
First published in paperback by Collins in 1997
1 3 5 7 9 8 6 4 2

Collins is an imprint of HarperCollins Publishers Ltd,
77/85 Fulham Palace Road, London W6 8JB

ISBN 000-675-321-3

Printed and bound in Great Britain by
Clays Ltd, St Ives plc

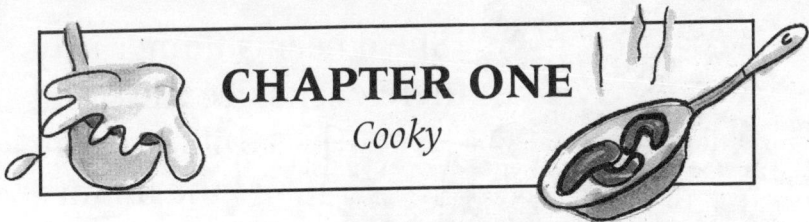

CHAPTER ONE
Cooky

Cooky (or Mrs Cookson to give her full name) was famous at Greenfields School and all the children loved her. Why? Well to start with she'd been the school cook and dinner lady there for as long as anyone could remember.

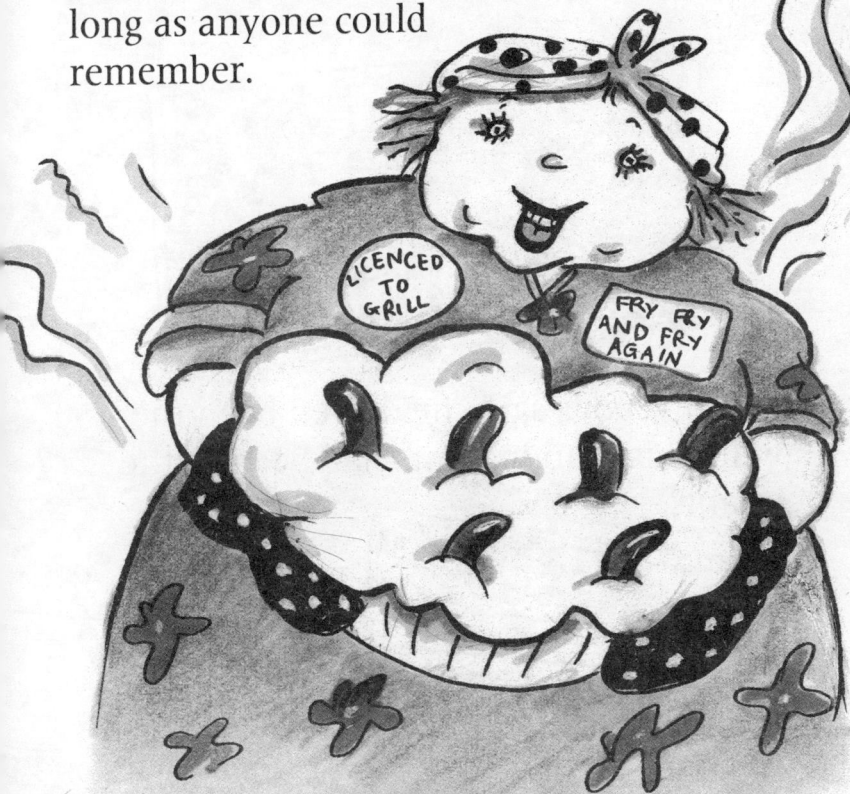

LICENCED TO GRILL

FRY FRY AND FRY AGAIN

She'd been a dinner lady there ever since Alice and Dilip were in the infants.

She'd been a dinner lady when Alice's mum and Dilip's dad were in the infants.

Kevin Woods said she'd even been there when his grandparents had been in the infants.

But that couldn't be possible. Could it?

Cooky had stuffed generations of
Greenfield children with her sizzling
sausages, her fresh green salads,
her crunchy chips and her
raspberry jam roly-poly. She was
a bit like a roly-poly herself –
round and soft and just
oozing
with sweetness.

She was the most cheerful person you
could imagine . . . and she was big.

Everything about her was big.

She had a big smile.

She had a BIG heart.

She had
a big VOICE

And she
gave you very BIG helpings.

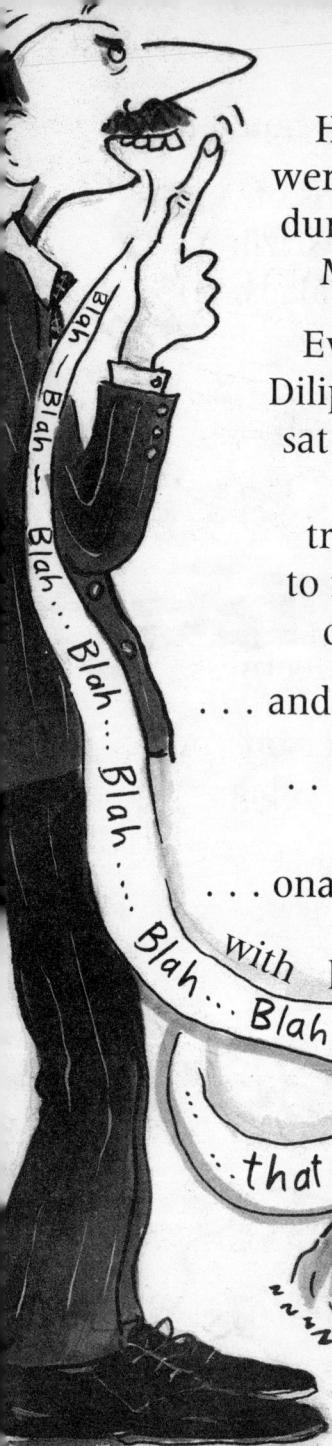

Her chatterings and clattering were always welcome especially during Mr McGeek's extra-long Monday morning assemblies.

Every Monday morning Alice, Dilip and the other 140 children sat on the hard hall floor trying not to shuffle their bottoms, trying not to fidget, trying not to fall asleep while Mr McGeek droned on and on and on. . .

. . . and on and on . . .

. . . and on and . . .

. . . onandonandonandon . . .

with his usual *in my young days . . .*

Blah — Blah — Blah . . . Blah . . . Blah . . . Blah . . . Blah . . . Blah . . .

and

. . . that reminds me of another story . . .

groan

But just as Alice, Dilip and the other 140 children had got to the point where they thought they would explode with silence and boredom, Cooky would arrive and, with a

RATTLE

and a

CLANG

open up the big metal shutters of her kitchen hatch. Then she would sail across the hall, her flowery overall billowing around her as she smiled and sang, patted heads and shrieked a cheery 'Good morning duckies' to everybody.

Mrs Cookson, please!

Mr McGeek would say,

I am trying to conduct an assembly!

Oh don't mind little me!

Cooky would bellow genially.

I'll just get on with my cooking.

Then her crew of dinner ladies would arrive and there'd be a clanging of pans, a rattling of cutlery and a squeaking of oven doors. It drowned out the school orchestra – which in the opinion of Alice and Dilip was no bad thing.

Then of course there were the songs.

Cooky loved to sing. She'd use well-known tunes and add her own dinner lady words. Her crew of assistants would back her up, clattering and rattling and joining in the choruses.

So if ever you were stuck in class, scratching your head and worrying about a particularly tricky sum, you could relax and listen to her version of 'I do like to be beside the seaside':

BANG

BONG

CLICK

Oh I do like to make a lot of custard
I do like to make an apple pie.
But I also like to make cod and haddock, chips and hake
And good hot stews and a chocolate cake!

Cooky would even announce the day's menu in song . . .

Today it's mince and scones...

. . . and clapping like a football crowd she'd chant:

2-4-6-8 - I've been cooking something great
10-12- and - 14
the yummiest pies you've ever seen!

Sometimes there'd be surprises like the day she sang her version of the Teddy Bears' Picnic:

She made lots of mistakes. She'd never got the hang of metric measures – everything she made turned out huge.

She made great steaming vats of custard,

rock cakes big as boulders

and huge towering mountains of mashed potato.

Once she made dumplings that swelled to such an enormous size that she couldn't squeeze them out of the kitchen hatch. The children just had to dive in.

She loved to bake – chunky cherry cakes, chocolate cakes, flapjacks and butterfly cakes as big as golden eagles. Her huge red arms seemed permanently plunged into dough or cake mix.

Wonderful whiffs of steamed apple and pie crusts and pink icing surrounded her.

Part of her job was to make sure the children behaved and ate nicely and, of course, she had her own special Cooky way of doing that.

She'd patrol the hall, helping the infants, joking with the juniors and singing out her dinner lady advice.

CHAPTER TWO
Cooking up a Storm

The day Mr McGeek announced that
Cooky and her crew were being replaced
was a sad day.

Cooky was sad.

Her crew was sad.

And the children
of Greenfields Primary School
were very sad indeed.

In fact they were in tears. Even Kevin
Woods who always said he was hard as
nails (and would never so much as blink
when he got kicked in football) – even he
was sniffing and saying he'd got
something in his eye.

Alice and Dilip were particularly miserable.

It won't be the same here without Cooky!

they moaned.

But Mr McGeek was jubilant. He'd always thought Cooky was too big, too loud, too . . . everything. He liked a nice quiet school.

I want this school to run like clockwork

he said.

Quiet and efficient. Efficient and quiet.

He loved to save money. So he was beaming when he announced:

We're getting a new ultra-modern bang-up-to-date cheap-to-run service!

We can't stand in the way of progress can we?

He shook Cooky's podgy hand and presented her with a going away present.

We hope you'll enjoy using this stainless-steel twin-purpose potato-masher and custard-lump squidger—

—and do feel welcome to pop in any time, any time that we have a fête or a concert or an open day.

And that was that.

Cooky and her crew packed up their overalls and their wooden spoons and trudged off home.

16

The next day the new ultra-modern bang-up-to-date cheap-to-run service arrived.

It was two thin ladies and a shiny metal wagon.

No more baking here!

they announced.

No more noise!

No more cooking smells!

Just quiet, efficient, healthy, cheap, modern food. Served to you at twelve on the dot.

17

The dinner trolley glided on very smoothly oiled wheels. Not a sound.

It was tightly sealed. Not a smell.

The two ultra-modern bang-up-to-date cheap-to-run dinner ladies were tall and very thin. Their skin was tight and as unnaturally pink as a raw sausage. They wore silver badges with 'Dinner Operative 1' and 'Dinner Operative 2' on them. Their white coats were tightly buttoned and stiff with starch. Their belts were firmly fastened with hard metal buckles.

On their heads they wore shiny white caps with very sharp peaks. They looked like two very bad-tempered seagulls.

If they bent down to talk to you they could give you a nasty peck with those peaks

said Alice.

Dilip shuddered.

They look as if they could do just about anything.

They look more like extra-terrestrials than dinner ladies

Kevin Woods complained.

Bring back Cooky is what I say.

19

At twelve o'clock the children gathered in the hall.

There was no sign of any dinner.

There were no smells of any dinner.

And there were no sounds at all.

No Cooky beaming and cheerily yodelling the menu. No dinner ladies yattering and clattering. Just two dinner operatives crackling with starch and one shiny metal trolley.

I want dumplings!

sighed Dilip.

I want chips!

sighed Kevin Woods.

I want Cooky back!

sighed Alice.

No talking!

barked bang-up-to-date Dinner Operative Number One.

Line up, single file!

shrieked cheap-to-run ultra-modern Number Two.

All our food is pre-packed and pre-served.

There is no choice. Line up and take one pack. No more. No less.

One by one each child collected their sealed pack of food.

"what is this?" whispered Alice.

SILENCE!

Back to your seats.

Await further instructions.

The puzzled children walked back to their places.

The diving into dumplings days seemed to be well and truly over.

"Quick march!" ordered Dinner Operative Number One.

No talking.

Sit up straight.

On the count of three open your packs...1-2-3-

22

The junior children opened their packs.

The infants stared miserably at theirs. Their little fat fingers couldn't get a good hold on the slippery packs.

On the count of three, tip contents into bowl... 1-2-3-

The juniors tipped out the contents.

The infants looked at each other and tried not to cry.

On the count of three eat... 1-2-3-

Come here that boy

barked Operative
Number One.

She wrote his name in a book.

This food, for your information, is extract of seaweed. Full of protein, very nourishing and very, very cheap. You will all eat exactly one bowlful before you leave.

Except Kevin Woods.

He will have seconds.

In the playground the infants were still starving and the juniors were feeling sick.

I can't eat that slime again

said Dilip.

I feel ill

said Alice.

I hope it's better tomorrow.

But tomorrow's glop was just as bad, only this time it was Yellow

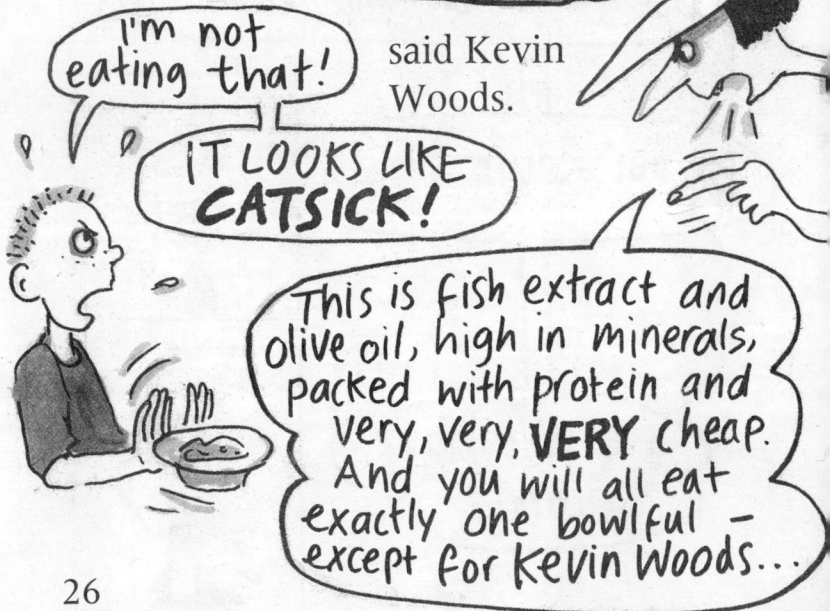

I'm not eating that!

said Kevin Woods.

IT LOOKS LIKE CATSICK!

This is fish extract and olive oil, high in minerals, packed with protein and very, very, **VERY** cheap. And you will all eat exactly one bowlful — except for Kevin Woods...

The next day the glop was **brown**.

No one had the heart to ask what it was.

All the children, including Kevin Woods, spooned it into their mouths and miserably filed out.

We've got to get Cooky back...

said Alice,
and Dilip and all the other children,
especially Kevin Woods, agreed.

...But how?

CHAPTER FOUR
Sizzling Surprise

In the staff room the teachers nibbled on shop-bought sandwiches and spooned strawberry yoghurt into their mouths. Only the supply teacher had the school dinners.

It looks very... ...healthy. she said doubtfully. The others agreed.

Might try it myself — tomorrow maybe... or the day after...

Or maybe next week.

Mr McGeek rubbed his hands with glee.

I am very pleased with my ultra-modern, cheap-to-run system.

It's so quiet here now. The children are silent and well-behaved. They are not eating that old-fashioned fattening food – and we're saving **POTS** of money!

PROFITS

EFFICIENCY PLAN

SCHOOL SAVINGS

We'll soon be able to buy all the new books and things you've been asking for.

All we need to do is convince the parents and the governors at tomorrow's concert. Then we can keep this new dinner system **for ever!**

Kevin Woods spent most playtimes standing outside the staff room waiting to be told off about something. Today was no exception and so he had overheard everything.

Keep this new system for ever? **NO WAY!**

As soon as he could he went off to spread the news.

We've got to do something

said Alice.

What about a protest?

WE WANT COOKy back!

We Want dumplings

DINNER OPERATIVES Go HOME

'What about a strike?' suggested Dilip.

NO FOOD No WORK

'What about kidnapping the new dinner operatives and holding them to ransom until we get Cooky back?' suggested Kevin Woods.

'Hey, we don't have to do anything,' said Dilip. 'When Mr McGeek shows these new dinners to our mums and dads, they'll be on our side.'

'One taste of the glop and all the parents will be saying "Bring back Cooky." Just wait and see. No Problem.'

£ £ £ £ £ £

But the next night Mr McGeek gave out lists of figures and thick booklets all explaining what a good thing the new ultra-modern bang-up-to-date cheap-to-run system was. And one by one the parents were giving in.

It says here 'scientific!'

That sounds good.

You can't stand in the way of progress.

Several parents nodded.

All those old-fashioned foods are very fattening.

Several chubby mums agreed.

This food is well-balanced... nutritious and...

... totally disgusting!

COST OF FOOD CHART: SEPT. — JULY

Of course it takes **some** children a little time to get used to new ideas.

But I'm sure you'll agree it's all for the best.

We've already saved a considerable amount of money which we have used to pay for new maths equipment.

The governors and parents applauded.

We don't actually have any food for you to taste...

I wonder why!

muttered Kevin Woods.

...but I'm sure you'd be interested in seeing the new system. So here to show it to you are our new ultra-modern bang-up-to-date cheap-to-run catering operatives.

The trolley glided in soundlessly.

Behind it stood the two new dinner ladies gleaming with cleanliness and efficiency. They swung the trolley open and proudly displayed the contents.

Inside were huge squeezy tubes of glop.
Only you couldn't see the glop because it
was in sealed containers with
labels like:

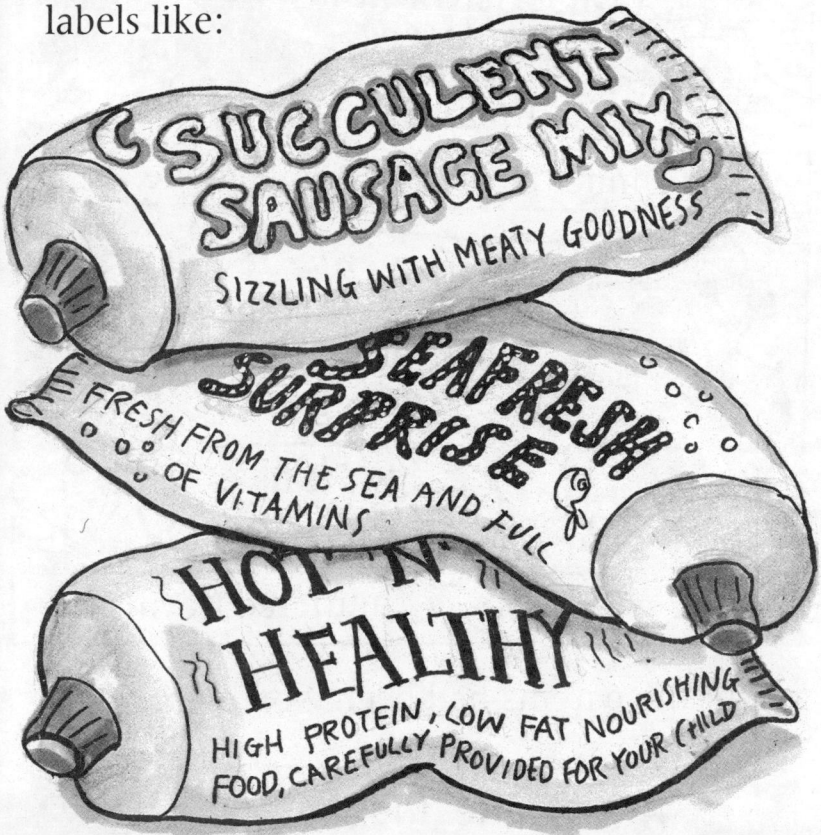

SUCCULENT SAUSAGE MIX

SIZZLING WITH MEATY GOODNESS

SEAFRESH SURPRISE

FRESH FROM THE SEA AND FULL OF VITAMINS

HOT 'N' HEALTHY

HIGH PROTEIN, LOW FAT NOURISHING FOOD, CAREFULLY PROVIDED FOR YOUR CHILD

There were also jars with pictures of
children licking their lips and smiling. The
words NEW!, SCIENTIFICALLY
BALANCED and NOURISHING were
splashed all over the gaily coloured packs.

said Dinner Operative Number One.

muttered Kevin.

But the parents had been won over.

Alice, Dilip, Kevin Woods and the other juniors were keeping an eye on this.

Now what can we do?

sighed Alice.

We're **DOOMED!**

said Kevin.

Doomed to eating ooze and sludge and glop and gunge...

...and having **extra maths** as a reward!

sighed Dilip.

He loved dumplings and hated long division so things looked especially bleak for him. It all seemed hopeless.

Absolutely hopeless.

Amongst the crowds of
parents, governors and
visitors milling about
waiting for the concert
to start, the children
spotted a familiar figure.
It was Cooky. She was
gazing wistfully at her
locked and bolted
kitchen hatch and
sighing.

Then she saw the children.

Hello duckies! she said.

Just visiting. Mr McGeek said I could drop in for concerts and the like.

Thought I'd just have a last look at my kitchen.

She sighed again.
Her chins wobbled.

They joined her at the kitchen. The hatch was firmly locked but the door . . . was not.

Keep watch —

instructed Kevin Woods.

—We're going in.

Ooh should we? wondered Dilip but it was too late. Quick as a ferret Kevin was in and hissing to the others to follow him.

It was no longer the warm and whiffy kitchen Cooky had run.

It was **COLD** and **SHINY**

highly polished and empty.

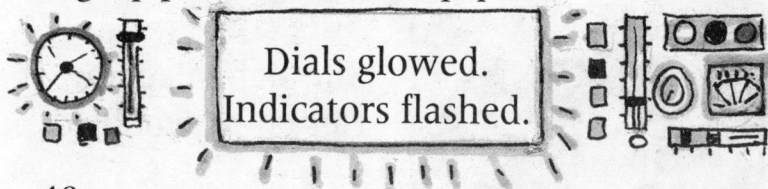

Dials glowed.
Indicators flashed.

Looks more like a spaceship than a kitchen, don't it duckies?

sighed Cooky.

Spooky!

said Alice.

But Kevin Woods liked it. He loved computers and machines. He loved pressing buttons and pulling levers. He stroked a control board.

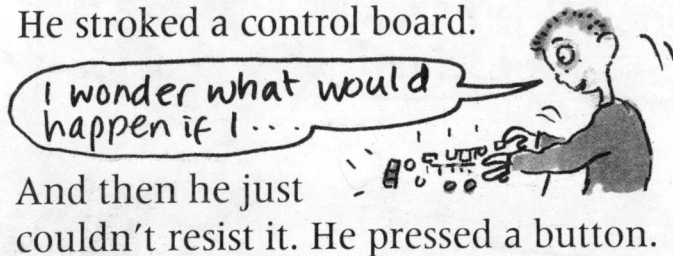

I wonder what would happen if I...

And then he just couldn't resist it. He pressed a button.

WHIRRRR

SQUEEK! EEEEK!

and YOW!

Strange noises came from the hall. Alice poked her head out of the door to have a look.

Dinner Operative Number One had bent her head rather suddenly.

She's given the school secretary a nasty peck with her cap peak – I said they looked sharp didn't I?

Kevin was still fiddling with knobs and switches.

Suddenly Dinner Operative Two stood to attention and shouted:

Line up. Dinner will be served!

The parents looked puzzled. A few of them shuffled into an uneasy line. The others gazed at each other in bewilderment.

"So that's why they're so cheap to run..." said Cooky.

"You can turn them off when you don't need 'em and you don't have to pay 'em at all!"

"They seem to be pre-programmed" said Kevin.

"But we can soon change that."

And he pressed lots of buttons and switches at once.

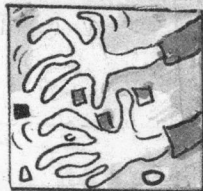

Click, click, click, lights FLASHED and FIZZED.
Click, click, click, puffs of smoke began to rise from the control panel.

Click, click, BANG!

The system went into overload.

CHAPTER SIX
Dinner is Served

In the hall most of the grown-ups were lined up. Some were standing straight and tall, trying to give a good example to the others. A few were messing about and talking at the back. Two mums blushed and giggled nervously then fell silent and looked guilty.

Sorry, Miss.

Hee Hee

they muttered when they realised the eyes of the dinner operatives were on them.

Both operatives were now barking orders.
But the orders were strangely mixed up.

Single line!

they barked.

File up!

On the count of three, **SIT**. 1-2-3-

Sit up straight.

No standing.

NOW QUICK MARCH. 1-2-3-

Some of the more obedient parents had
sat down.

Now they attempted to shuffle forwards
on their bottoms.

It's a bit like aerobics!

giggled one of the mums.

SILENCE! screamed Dinner Operative Two.

There is NO choice!

She was clutching a mega squeezy tube of Seafresh Surprise and counting 1 2 3 as she waltzed around with it.

Number One Operative was opening and closing the trolley, picking up packets and putting them down, nodding and barking out orders at the same time. Suddenly, she stopped, stood up straight, marched forward and flung both her arms out wide.

It was at that very moment that Dinner
Operative Two, clutching the mega
squeezy tube of Seafresh Surprise span in
her direction.

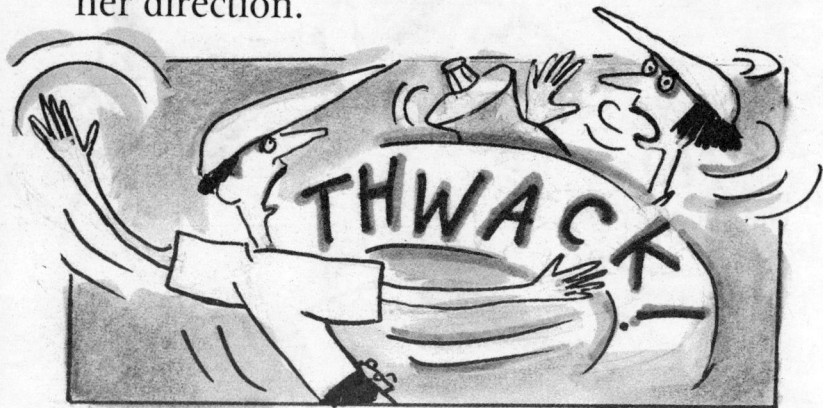

THWACK!

The arms of Operative One collided with
the tube held by Operative Two and

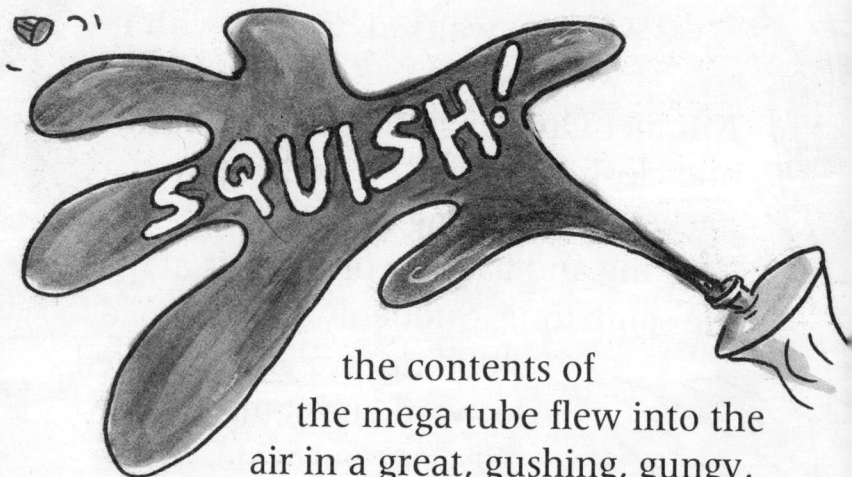

SQUISH!

the contents of
the mega tube flew into the
air in a great, gushing, gungy,
green fountain.

Dinner is served

she announced.

Parental eyes peered up at the sight.

The somewhat slower parental brains began to realise what would happen and then . . . parental bodies scattered to get out of the way.

Too late. The fountain of Seafresh Surprise fell on to their upturned faces. It oozed down their noses and plopped on to their clothes. Green and gloppy parents stood and gasped.

YUCK!

said the one or two unlucky ones who'd got a mouthful of the gunge.

Have you tasted this stuff?

It's revolting!

Good Heavens!

said Mr McGeek and he set off towards the kitchen to do something about it. But he hadn't gone far before he stepped on a particularly slimy bit of Seafresh Surprise and skidded sideways into Dinner Operative One, sending her into a mad spin.

She began to fling packets left, right and high above her as she span. Meanwhile Operative Two was picking up another mega tube.

This time it was Succulent Sausage Mix that flew into the air.

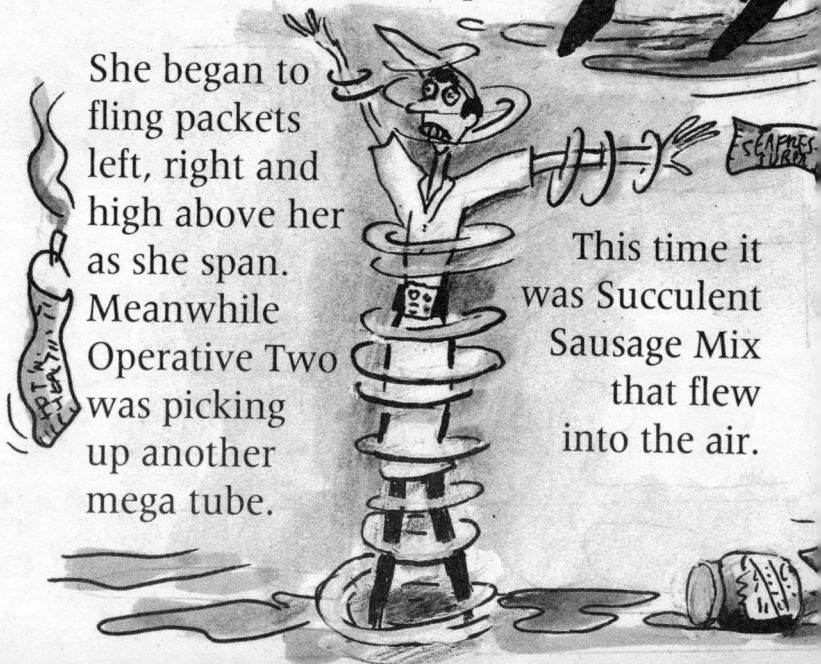

A particularly large blob of pink sludge plopped on to the bald head of Mr McGeek.

Then it all got out of control. The school secretary slid into the lollipop lady, the lollipop lady turned and accidentally thwacked the caretaker with her lollipop, the caretaker lost his temper and

It was the food fight to end all food fights.

It was mayhem.

It was madness.

It was marvellous.

Several parents felt the
urge to join in.

Many more were involved by
accident as they slipped in slime
and collided with others, pushing
them into the puddles of pink and
green ooze that Operative Two
was adding to all the time.

I didn't mean to...   they wailed.

It was an accident,
honest!

It wasn't my
fault... it
was **her**!

The Juniors were quick to join in. They
slid and squidged and made mounds of
Sizzling Sausage Mix snowballs which
they lobbed cheerfully at each other.

The only ones
who maintained their common
sense were the infants who
were still sitting cross-legged
and wide-eyed with their
teacher Miss Sweetie.
They were all dressed in their
concert outfits. Some were
sheep. Some were cows.
The rest were stalks of corn,
trees and bushes. They
gazed in awe at the big
children and the parents
and the governors going
mad all around them.

They're getting over-excited

said one perceptive
five year old.

They looked to Miss Sweetie for instruction. But she was too busy thinking about her new silk shirt and trying to keep well out of the way of a particularly large squidge of Hot 'n' Healthy that was coming towards her.

She wondered what to do. Maybe she should keep her infants busy and distracted. Perhaps a lovely little song?

She considered improvising:

Ten green mummies sliding round the floor
Ten green mummies sliding round the floor
But if one green mummy should squidge out of the door
There'd be nine green mummies sliding on the floor.

Or maybe they could count the grown-ups as they toppled. Several of the infants could count as far as fifteen and they were always glad to show off their skills.

The glop of Hot 'n' Healthy landed

dangerously near her new silk blouse and a third option occurred to her.

I'll just pop into the P.E. alcove and check on the apparatus…

she said and legged it.

The abandoned infants blinked at each other. What were they supposed to do now?

A couple dipped their hands into the green and yellow ooze surrounding them and started a very exciting finger-painting pattern.

Miss Sweetie would have been proud of them – had she not been hiding behind the bean bags.

The other infants, still doubtful, remembered their teacher's good advice: 'When in doubt, see what the grown-ups do and try to act like them.'

So they stood up and, working nicely and quietly in twos, they toured the hall one politely squeezing blobs of glop out of a tube while the other took very careful aim.

Soon they started to hurl and slide and shout and scream – just like the grown-ups.

WHOOSH!

SLIDE

It was all over in twelve minutes. But what a twelve minutes!

Parents shimmied and slipped and splished and sploshed.

Children shrieked and screamed and in the middle of it all, the two stiff and starchy dinner operatives spun like breakdancers, barking out nonsense and flinging more and more food into the fight.

CHAPTER EIGHT
Tea and Biscuits

Unfortunately all good things come to an end. Eventually the two dinner operatives ran out of power.

Their orders became slower.

Their voices deepened and ground to a halt.

Their whirling subsided.

They stopped. Stood stiffly to attention.

Counted 1 2 3.

And then they simply fell over.

PING

WHIRZ

After a while the food fight drew to a close. One by one, baffled and embarrassed parents realised what they'd been doing. They blinked, rubbed their eyes and tried to make excuses.

Well I didn't start it...

Several parents were clearly exhausted by their unaccustomed exercise. They sat slumped and bedraggled in various puddles of ooze.

PANT

SWEAT

Mr McGeek felt he ought to do something to calm the agitated and revive the exhausted – but what . . . ?

What shall I do? What shall I do?

he muttered.

Fortunately, Cooky had the answer.

She sailed out of the kitchen bearing a tray of cups, a mountain of biscuits and an enormous teapot.

What we all need . . .

she boomed,

. . . is a nice cup of tea . . .

Ah the gentle
voice of reason

said the Chairman
of the Governors,
rising from his puddle
of Seafresh Surprise.

Thank goodness
you're still with
us, Mrs Cookson.

Mr McGeek, for once reduced to silence,
stood and dripped quietly. Then he
gathered his few remaining senses,
coughed and whispered:

You will
come back,
Mrs Cookson?

Oh I think we can talk about that, Duckie.

Cooky beamed.

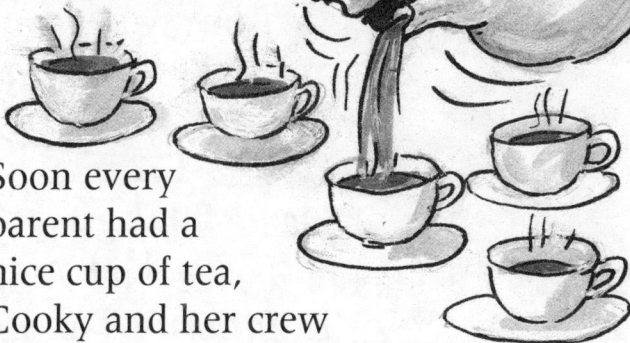

Soon every parent had a nice cup of tea, Cooky and her crew had their jobs back and Alice, Dilip, Kevin Woods and all the other children had huge smiles on their faces.

So we'll leave them there with Cooky still pouring out gallons of tea from her enormous teapot, the tea frothing and bubbling, the teaspoons tinkling and the hearty tones of Cooky singing as she hands round more biscuits.